Patr IR

Outback Rescue

DARREL and
SALLY ODGERS

Illustrated by
JANINE DAWSON

D0360318

For Barry Odgers (Joe);
our brother and friend.
- Darrel and Sally O

For Barb - Janine Dawson

First American Edition 2017
Kane Miller, A Division of EDC Publishing

Text copyright © Sally and Darrel Odgers 2015
Cover copyright © Scholastic Australia 2015
Internal illustrations copyright © Janine Dawson 2015
First published by Scholastic Press a division of Scholastic Australia Pty Limited in 2015.
Cover illustration by Heath McKenzie
This edition published under license from Scholastic Australia Pty Limited

For information contact:
Kane Miller, A Division of EDC Publishing
PO Box 470663
Tulsa, OK 74147-0663
www.kanemiller.com
www.edcpub.com
www.usbornebooksandmore.com

Library of Congress Control Number: 2016959844

Printed and bound in the United States of America

1 2 3 4 5 6 7 8 9 10

ISBN: 978-1-61067-656-4

Dear Readers,

My name is **Barnaby Station Stamp of Approval**, but you can call me Stamp. My friend Ace and I travel around the country with James Barnaby in a vehicle we call the **Fourby**. I am a **border collie**, so you won't be surprised to learn that I am handsome and clever. Ace isn't a border collie, but she's clever, too. James likes making friends with other people and other dogs. He talks a lot, especially to Ace and me.

The story you are about to read is our fourth big Pup Patrol adventure. After the Great Atherton K9 Festival, we were planning to head into the outback. But the road James wanted to take was closed so we ended up going somewhere else . . . And it was just as well we did!

Yours,

Stamp

Pup Patroller

Who's Who.

The Crew of the Fourby

James Barnaby. James is 19. He wants to be a vet.

Barnaby Station Stamp of Approval. Me. A clever, handsome border collie.

Ace. A dog of mixed breed, bad manners and great loyalty.

Other Family and Friends

Dad and Mum Barnaby. James's parents back at Barnaby Station.

At Billabong Camp

Bobby Corella. A young man at Camp Billabong.

Mick. Bobby's dad.

Grandad. Bobby's grandfather.

Burnu. Top dog at Camp Billabong.

Girra. Burnu's mate. Alpha female at Camp Billabong.

Murana. A young camp dog.

In the outback

Elsa and Fritz Mueller. Tourists from Germany.

Stamp's Glossary

Barnaby Station Stamp of Approval.
Pedigreed animals often have long names.
My parents are named Barnaby Station Penny
Black and Brightwood Superlative.
Border collies. Herding dogs that came from
the Anglo-Scottish borders. They are one of the
most intelligent dogs in the world.
The Fourby. Four-wheel drive SUV.

Chapter One

Way Out West

"I smell something," said Ace. She drilled her sharp little nose into the ground and sniffed. Then she sneezed so hard her ears waggled.

I just said, "**Of-paws** you do. You smelled it earlier. So did I." I should have been more alert because Ace is *really* good at tracking. She has mixed terrier ancestry. I am a herding dog, which means I rely a lot on my eyes and ears.

Ace started off the dusty track and into some long grass. "It's going this way," she reported. "Oh, here it is—wiggly thing—"

That's when I heard a dry rustle in the grass. "Stop!" I dashed forward and grabbed Ace by the scruff of the neck. Of-paws she twisted around and bit my elbow.

I yelped and let her go. Ace turned and launched herself at my ear, latching on with her sharp teeth.

So, why were Ace and I fighting in the long grass? Ace was doing it because she's mostly terrier and that's what terriers do. As for me, I had a very good reason to grab her. But let's go back to the beginning of the story.

It all started when we left Atherton Tops after the Great K9 Festival. James went into a service station on the outskirts of Cairns. "No point in going right into the city," he said to Ace and me when he came back. "I already stocked up with supplies back at Atherton."

Ace panted, her tongue dangling to her paws. "Too hot," she said to me.

I agreed.

James unfolded the map and ran his

finger over the top part. It was getting crumpled and messy. We'd been using it since we started our travels. "Um . . . um . . . um . . ." he muttered.

"Why's he doing that?" asked Ace.

"He's deciding where to go," I said.

"Normanton and the Gulf," announced James. "Way out west." He folded up the map and looked pleased.

I wagged the end of my tail. James was happy. When the pack leader is happy, so is the rest of the pack.

We drove west for a couple of days. James stopped the Fourby often so we could all get out and stretch our legs. When we made camp early on the second evening, James filled our bowls with **water** and used his **spirit stove** to make hot coffee. Then he went to the **HF radio** mounted on the Fourby to talk to Dad

Barnaby back home at Barnaby Station.

As soon as James turned his back, Ace sneaked over to where he had left his coffee on a flat rock. She sniffed it loudly.

"Coffee isn't good for dogs," I warned her. "Besides, it tastes bad."

"How do *you* know?" said Ace. She sniffed the mug again.

"I tasted some when I was a pup," I

explained. "Trust me. It tastes terrible and you'll burn your tongue."

Ace backed away, then trotted over to the Fourby. I followed her.

"We're heading west, Dad," James was saying. "Might see if there's any work out at Normanton. Over."

"You're certainly seeing a lot of the country," said Dad Barnaby. "Over."

"You should fly up and travel with us for a bit," said James. "Over."

"I wish I could . . . listen, James, be careful on your way west. I've been watching the news and a couple of tourists are missing somewhere out there. They were heading east from Perth—the authorities think they must have detoured because of the flooding after the cyclone. Over."

"We won't go missing," said James. "We're on a main road and you know I'm always careful. Over."

James ended the call. "Poor old Dad," he said to Ace and me. "He's always worrying about something. First he thought we might get caught up in a bushfire and then he was worried about us getting mixed up in a cyclone . . . oh." He laughed.

Oh, indeed, I thought. We *did* get mixed up with a bushfire and a cyclone! It had been a long time since I last saw Mum and Dad Barnaby, and my own mum, too. "What was your mum like?" I asked Ace.

Ace stared at me. "I don't remember." Then she headed back to sniff at James's cooling cup of coffee, just in case.

"Ace, stop that!" called James.

Ace **smarled**.

Stamp's Glossary

HF radio. High frequency radio. James's radio is not the kind that plays music. It's the kind people use to talk to one another.

Of-paws. Of course, for dogs.

Smarl. A dog grin. Some dogs smarl a lot. Some don't do it at all.

Spirit stove. A small stove that campers use when it isn't safe to light a fire.

Water. At home, water comes out of a faucet. When traveling in the outback, it's impawtant to carry lots of water.

A Word on Breed Behavior

Different breeds of dog have what we call **breed characteristics**. This means they are more likely to do some things if they are a certain type of dog. Herding dogs like me like to round up sheep and cattle. Sometimes we round up ducks or children if there are no sheep around! Spaniels like to jump into rivers or lakes because they were bred to work in water. Terriers are quick and nippy because they were bred as hunters and ratters.

Chapter Two
Off the Road

Driving west across the **Top End** was exciting because of all the new smells. At the same time, it was dull because the road was as straight as an arrow and we sometimes seemed to look at the same view for hours.

I was dozing when I realized the Fourby had gone around a bend and suddenly came to a stop. A van was parked by the road while two men put up a stop sign. A metal gate stretched across the road, blocking the way.

James stuck his head out the window. "Good afternoon!" he called.

One of the men tipped back his hat and walked over. "Where are you headed, mate?"

"West, to the Gulf," said James. "Why?"

"There's pretty extensive flooding out this way after the cyclone," said the man. "We're advising people to head back east until the road's passable."

"Oh," said James. "Any idea how long before we can get through?"

"A few days." The man shrugged. He looked across to the passenger seat where I was sitting in my harness. "Nice lookin' border, mate!"

"Thanks," said James.

The man stepped back, nearly tripping when Ace yapped at him through her window. "Where did you get the yapper?" "We chose her down in Victoria," said

James. "She's a **conglomerate terrier**."

The other man went *hmph!* from where he stood by the stop sign. "Never saw the point of pets myself. Some people treat 'em better than they treat people. Anyway, you'd better turn back, son."

James turned the Fourby around without a word. I sensed he didn't like the second man much.

We drove back around the bend and along the road. Then he shook his head. "Huh! Fancy saying something like that to someone who clearly *does* see the point of pets? So rude!" He was obviously still cross about the man at the stop sign.

"Where are we going now?" asked Ace.

James pulled over to the side of the road again. He got out his map and ran his finger along it a little way. "Let's take the turnoff to Wahwee Creek," he said to us. "We'll find a camping spot in there. I don't want to drive right back to Cairns."

I pricked up my ears. If we were going to camp until the water went down, we'd have time for exploring. We might even make new friends, although we hadn't seen anyone apart from the signpost men for a while.

The road was rough and dusty, but Ace and I stuck our noses out through our windows to take in the scents. The wind carried the smell of tropical trees and warm animals. There was also the faint smell of brackish water from the floods. After a while, we saw trees up ahead and then a few small buildings.

"That can't be Wahwee Creek," said James. "We haven't come far enough."

"Dogs!" Ace suddenly yapped.

"Hens!" She started scrabbling with her front paws at the window ledge. "Hen-hen-hen-hen! Hen-feather-hen!"

"Don't even think about it, Ace," I said.

"Want to go **henning**," insisted Ace.

I felt my own paws twitch. It was a while since I'd had the chance to work

with sheep. Maybe hens would do instead.
I wouldn't hunt, hurt or hassle them, of-
paws. I'd just round them up a bit. They
wouldn't mind . . . much.

Stamp's Glossary

Conglomerate terrier. "Conglomerate"
means lots of things mixed together. This
is the best way to describe Ace.
Henning. Henning is like rabbiting or
ratting, only with hens. It's not a thing a
good dog would do.
Top End. The far north of Australia.

Chapter Three
Billabong Camp

James slowed the Fourby as we drove through the buildings. It didn't look much like a town. It was more like a camp. We saw some children playing kick-the-can. Others splashed in a **billabong**. I could hear them **cooeeing** and laughing even over all the noise Ace was making. Hens clucked and pottered around, and a couple of **corellas** looked down from a gum tree.

When James saw three men sitting

under the tree, he pulled over. One of them grinned out from under his shady hat. "G'day mate."

"G'day," replied James. "This isn't Wahwee Creek, is it?"

"No, that's way up there." The youngest man pointed inland.

"We just call this the **billabong camp**," said the eldest man. "You want to stay a while, boy? We're having a big cook-up tonight. Plenty of tucker for everyone."

"Thanks! Sounds good," said James. "We're heading west, but the main road's closed. I'm looking for somewhere to camp until it's open again."

"Stay here if you like," offered the first man. "You got a tent? Or you can bunk in with the boys."

"We have a tent, thanks." James got out of the Fourby. "I've got a couple of dogs, too. Is it okay if I let them out for a run?"

"Sure," said the youngest man. "We've got **camp dogs** here, but they won't bother yours. I'm Bobby Corella."

"Corella?"

"Like those fellas up there." Bobby grinned and pointed up to the white-and-red birds in the tree.

"I'm James Barnaby," said James. "The dogs are Stamp and Ace. Stamp's okay with other dogs, but Ace—"

"That the one hollering in the back?" asked Bobby.

Ace was still scrabbling and yapping about hens.

"That's her," said James. "Be quiet, Ace!" He turned back to the men. "She's still getting used to other dogs, sorry."

"Ah, let her out," said the eldest man. "She'll be right."

Bobby waved at the Fourby. "Go ahead, James. If Grandad says she'll be right, she'll be right."

"I hope so," said James. He opened the front door and let me out first. My paws itched to start herding hens, but I knew James wanted me to set **a good example**. I had a stretch and then sat down while he let Ace out. I saw him pick up Ace's leash, but as soon as he unclipped her harness, she shot out of the Fourby window like a cork out of a bottle. James dashed around and made a grab for her, but she pranced away, yapping.

"Hen-hen-hen! Hen-feather-hen!"

A big brown hen that had been clucking and scratching in the dust saw Ace coming and squawked, then sprinted off down towards the billabong. Ace sped after her.

James dashed after Ace. "Get her, Stamp!" he called.

I was happy to obey. Ace can't help being mostly terrier, but terriers don't *have* to be terrier-able all the time. Besides, it's rude to chase hens that don't belong to you.

Behind us, I heard Bobby's grandad laughing and saying, "She'll be right."

The hen cackled madly and flapped her wings. Up she went in the air like a mad feather duster. Then down she came again.

"Ace!" yelled James.

"Ace!" I barked.

"Wark! Warrrrrk!" yelled the hen. "Dog-dog-dog!"

"Hen-hen-hen!" **yaffled** Ace.

"Enough," said a voice, quite softly. And Ace stopped as if someone had grabbed her by the tail.

Stamp's Glossary

Billabong. An outback water hole.
Billabong camp. Some indigenous Australians live in camps and settlements built on traditionally owned land in remote Australia.
Camp dogs. Dogs with dingo ancestry.
Cooee. A loud shout.
Corella. A cockatoo with a short helmet-shaped crest.
A good example. Behaving well so that others learn to behave as well.
Yaffle. Noisy yapping and barking. Small dogs do this when they are overexcited.

Chapter Four

Burnu and Girra

For a moment I couldn't see who had spoken, but then two dogs stood up from where they'd been resting in the long, dry grass and stretched. Both were sandy colored, which was why I hadn't seen them right away. They weren't much bigger than me, but there was something different about them . . . I dropped my tail.

Ace stared at them for a second, then started to yaffle again. She darted up to the dogs and yapped in their faces. This is terrier-ably bad manners, but she was overexcited.

"Ace!" I snapped. "Stop that! This is their territory." I was frightened for her. If these dogs attacked, we'd both be in real trouble.

The bigger dog stared at Ace as if he'd never seen such a thing before. "I said, *that's enough*, small one."

"Calm yourself," said the other dog. She pushed Ace's head with her paw.

Ace snarled and then squeaked. "Let me up!"

"*Calm*," said the dog again. "When you are calm, I'll let you up."

I whined, unsure of what to do. I should probably **submit** to these dogs, I thought, but then that would have suggested I was too scared to defend Ace.

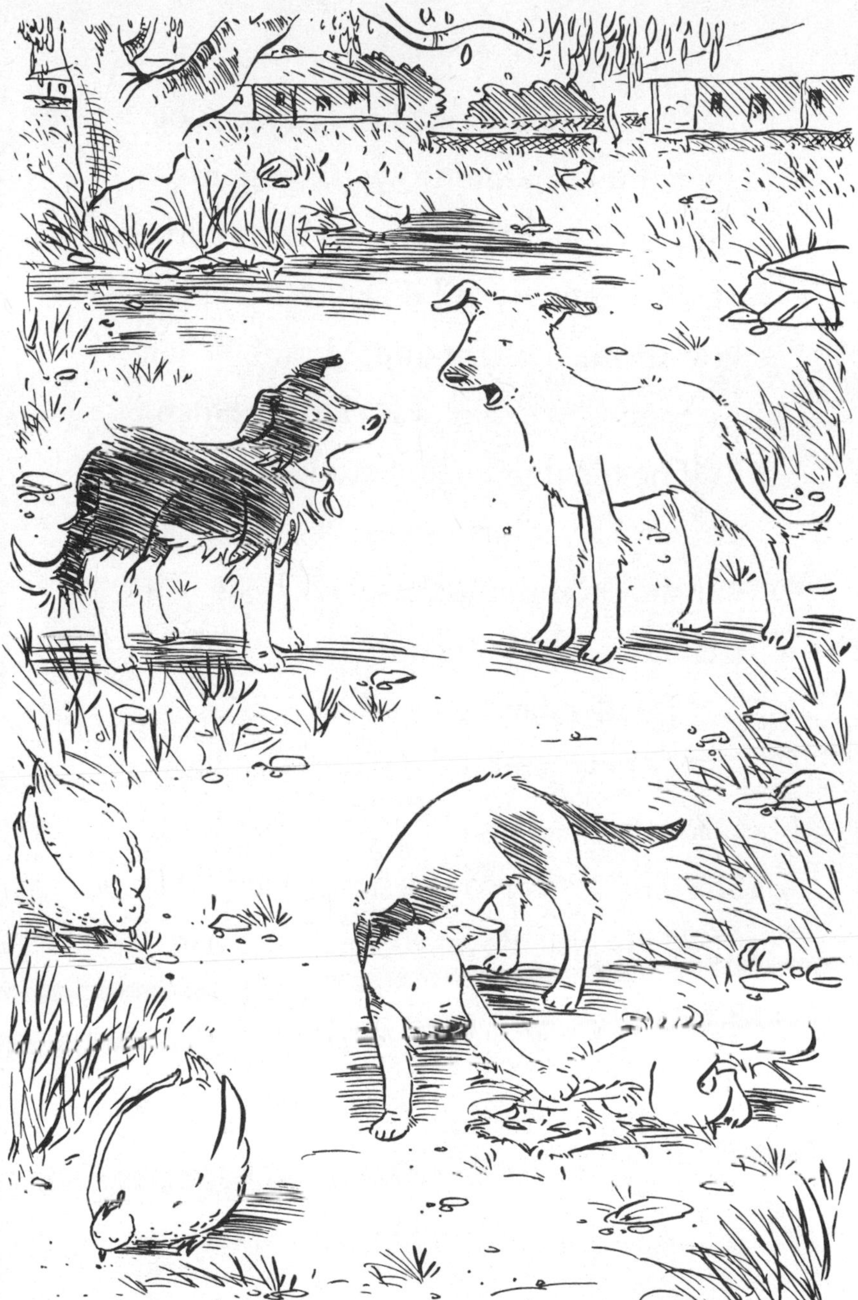

I had a good look at the bigger dog. His tail was up, but it wasn't wagging stiffly. I thought that meant he wouldn't attack. I kept my tail down in **neutral pawsition**. "I am Stamp," I said. "That is my friend, Ace. She was chasing a hen."

The big dog looked at me steadily with amber-colored eyes. "I know that. But she should not chase our hens. They are under my protection."

"I understand," I said.

"Good," said the big dog. He looked across to his mate. "Let her up, Girra. She will not chase our hens again." He tilted his gaze down to Ace, who had given up squirming and lay with her chin in the dust. "Will you, small one?"

Ace said nothing.

The dog called Girra lifted her paw and Ace bounced to her feet. "Hen-hen-

hen!" she shrilled, but then she sat down and sneezed, pawing at her nose.

"No hen," said Girra.

She sounded calm and the big dog had sat down, so I thought the danger was over, if only Ace behaved.

"I am Stamp," I said again. "I am top dog of the Fourby pack, but I know this is your territory."

"I am Burnu," said the big dog. "My mate is Girra."

Ace shook her hair out of her eyes. "Are you dingoes?"

"No," said Burnu. "The dingoes are our wild brothers and sisters. We are called camp dogs because we choose to live in the camps and communities."

"You belong to Bobby?" asked Ace.

"We belong to no one," said Burnu. "We live *with* the people, not for them."

"Bobby is our friend," Girra added. "But he is young, like a pup. Grandad is our equal."

"I see," I said. I was uneasy because all the dog packs I knew had a human alpha.

Girra moved her tail just a little. "It need not concern you, Stamp of the Fourby Pack," she said. "We have our ways and they are good. You have your ways and they are good."

"But *not* if they include henning with someone else's hens," said Burnu sternly to Ace.

"You may hen in your territory, but not in ours," added Girra gently.

Ace sulked. "But we don't *have* any hens in our territory."

"Is that so?" said Girra. "What territory has no hens?"

"It's complicated," I said. I explained

that we were traveling with James and so our territory was really just the Fourby and wherever we camped. "When we go home to Barnaby Station, it will be different," I said. "There are hens there, although Mum Barnaby doesn't approve of henning."

Girra and Burnu looked at each other and made some silent agreement.

"You may wander freely in our territory while you are here," said Burnu.

"But you may *not* go henning," Girra pointedly said to Ace.

Ace cast a wistful glance at the hen, who was clucking smugly over by the billabong. Then she looked up at me. "Here comes James," she said. "Let's go."

I wagged my thanks to the camp dogs and we trotted back to meet James. I had a lot to think about.

Stamp's Glossary

Neutral pawsition. A dog's tail tells a lot about the dog's mood. A neutral tail (low but relaxed) means wary but friendly.

Submitting. Junior dogs roll over to show their bellies to senior dogs. It's a way of saying, "You are above me in the pack order."

Chapter Five
Outback Bulldust

James patted me when we came up to him. "Well done, Stamp."

Then he turned to Ace. "As for you—I wish you would listen! But I think Grandad Corella was right. Those other dogs put you in your place without hurting you, right?"

Ace smarled at James and wiggled until he picked her up.

We had a great time at Camp

Billabong. After Burnu and Girra gave us **pawmission** to range around, we explored. The rest of the camp dogs were as still and calm as their pack leaders. Even the half-grown pups were quiet. They played, as pups do, but they listened when their elders gave them directions. Ace and I got to know them a bit, but none of them asked where we came from, or where we were going.

One of the younger dogs was Murana, which she said meant *willy wagtail*.

"Girra says I flit around like a silly bird," she told me. "She says I should learn to be still."

I suppose she was lively for a camp dog.

"What do you do here?" I asked.

"We hunt," she told me. "And we watch and listen. At night, we like to sing to the great wide dark."

Ace looked at me. "Stamp, I want to sing, please."

"Maybe we will sing tonight," said Murana. "If so, you may sing too, small one." She turned and loped off to drink at the billabong.

I found the camp dogs difficult to understand. With most dogs, it's easy to tell if they are friendly or grumpy, or if they want to play or to fight. My mum, Penny Black, taught me how to read dog signals when I was a tiny puppy. When I bit her

tail, she growled
and gave me a sharp little
nip. That's how I learned not to bite
other dogs. When she **play-bowed**, I
knew she was inviting me to play a game.

The camp dogs didn't signal much,
though. They just watched us for a few
seconds and then turned away as if we
weren't there. But I was sure they knew
exactly where we were and what we were
doing all the time.

The cook-up that night was fun.
We all sat around a campfire and ate

barbecued meat and a kind of **damper**. Ace and I had a big bone to gnaw on afterward, then Ace went off to play with some of the children. The moon came up and shone white light over us. The stars looked like spilled white sand. For a while it was quiet, and then we heard a long, low musical note.

"It's time to sing!" said Ace, leaping to her feet. In the moonlight, we saw the camp dogs flitting silently to the billabong. Murana passed us without a look, but I think she must have come

close deliberately so we could follow her.

In a few moments, we had joined the circle. All around us muzzles were raised to the sky and the song began. The camp dogs howled on different notes. It was pawfectly splendid.

We sang with them until suddenly they stopped and, without a word, slipped away in the moonlight. Ace and I went to sleep by James under the big gum tree.

In the morning, James took us to the billabong for a swim. The hens clucked around on the bank, but I noticed Ace stayed away from them. The big brown hen seemed to smirk at us.

After we got dry, James sat down under the corellas' tree with Grandad, his son Mick and Mick's son, Bobby. Ace went to play with the camp children, but I sat next to James.

"You can stay here as long as you like, James," said Mick. "No hurry, eh?"

"Not at all, but I don't know how long Ace will behave around all these hens," joked James.

"If you really need to move on, you could keep going on towards Wahwee Creek and then take the road to Karumba," said Mick. He picked up a stick and scratched some lines in the sand. "See, this is the five-way, but some of the tracks are just wallaby paths. You want to take this middle one. It's not the biggest, but it leads to *that* turnoff." He tapped one of the lines.

James leaned over to look. "Middle track. Right. What's the driving like? My dad said a couple of tourists got lost out this way."

"It's a big place, but you should be

okay. You won't run out of water after all the rain. Just watch out for the **bulldust**," said Bobby. "You get a lot of that here in the **outback** and there aren't many people around to help if you get into trouble."

"You got enough fuel for that bus?" Grandad nodded towards the Fourby.

"I fill up every chance I get and I carry an emergency supply," James said.

Grandad nodded. "Good. You go on then if you want. Been nice visiting."

"It's been great," said James. "Any tips on dealing with the bulldust?"

"Slow down and take it easy. Keep control of the steering and use four-wheel drive, and put your headlights on low beam in case something's coming the other way," said Mick. "Shouldn't be much, though, after the rain."

"Thanks." James got up and shook

hands with the three men. Then he packed up the Fourby and called to Ace. We were about to get in when Girra and Burnu appeared. I wasn't quite sure what they expected, so I waved my tail gently. They looked at me and Girra's tail moved just a bit. Ace got up on her hind legs and pranced her paws.

"Bye!" she said brightly to the camp dogs, then she darted away to the big tree. I saw her touch noses with Murana. "Bye, Murana."

"Good-bye, small one," said Murana.

Then Ace came back and pawed at the Fourby door. "Let's go."

A few minutes later, we had left Billabong Camp behind. I already missed our new friends, but it was good to get back on the road.

The road was narrow and a bit rough,

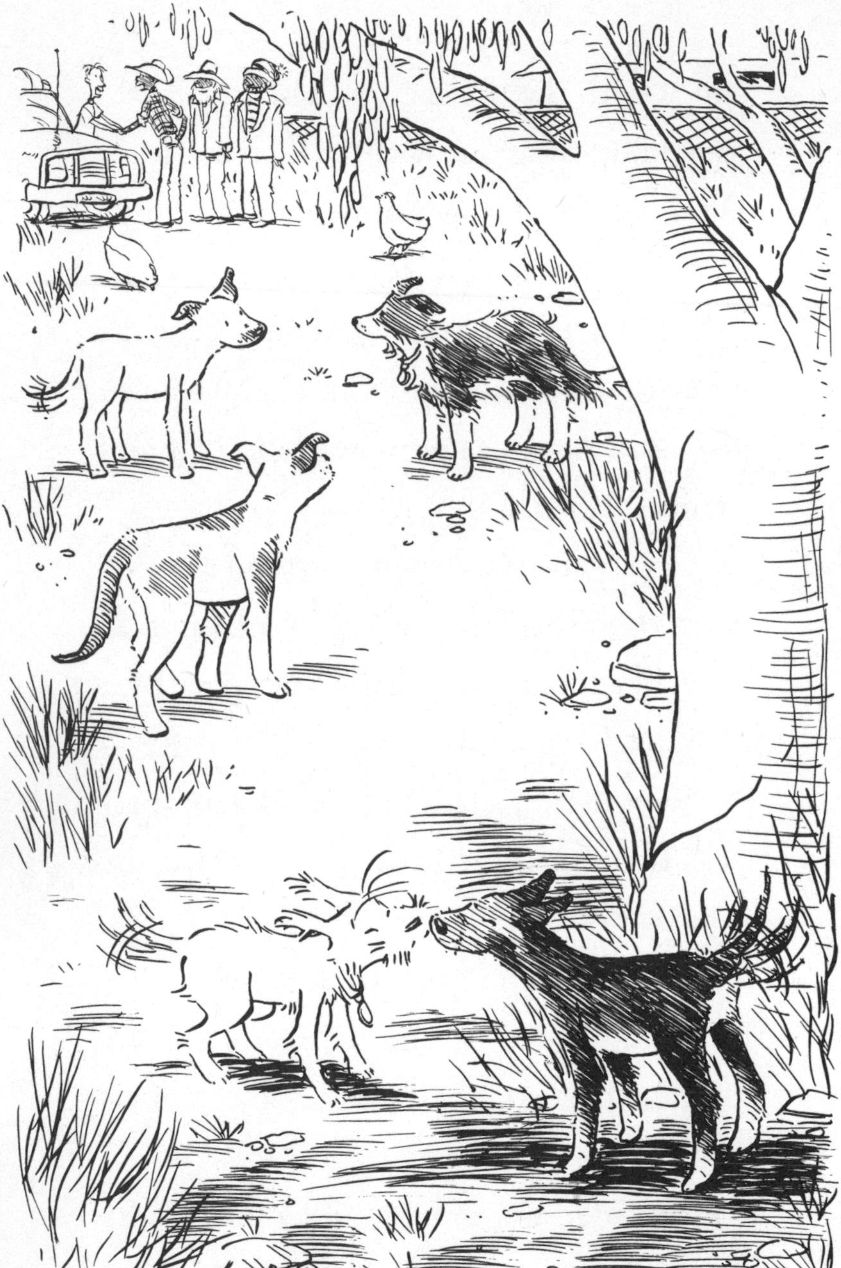

but the Fourby roared along. James sang along with the radio. We camped out that night under the stars and moved on early the next morning. We stopped at another water hole for a swim, and James put some more fuel in the Fourby and filled the empty water container.

Later that afternoon, James looked ahead at the road and said, "Uh-oh." I was sitting in the front seat and I looked out the windshield, too. The road did look strange, almost like sand after the tide goes out.

"Bulldust," said James. He repeated Mick's advice to himself. "Take it slowly, keep control of the steering and use four-wheel drive." He stopped and wound up all the windows. "Sorry, dogs. You don't want to be breathing in dust."

He started the Fourby again and drove

forward. As soon as we hit the bulldust, clouds of it rose in the air. The Fourby seemed to drift to one side, almost as if it was floating. "Oops," said James, and I saw him getting a tighter grip on the wheel. "Hope there's no big rocks under there."

The Fourby drifted to the other side and James pulled it to the edge of the road. "Big hole there," he said. The dust was all around us. It was like driving through a heavy cloud of smoke. I

remembered the smoke from the bushfire
back at Jasper and whined. "It's okay,
Stamp," said James. He corrected the
steering again and suddenly the Fourby
seemed to steady itself. It lurched and I
realized we were on firm road again.

James drove on for a bit. When the air
cleared, he stopped and wound down the
windows again.

"Phew! Hope there's not too much
bulldust up ahead," he said.

We all got out to stretch our legs.
When I looked behind us, the dust still
hung like clouds in the air.

Stamp's Glossary

Bulldust. Soft, powdery red dust that is difficult to drive through.

Damper. Bread baked in hot ashes or on a stick.

Outback. The less populated rural parts of Australia.

Pawmission. Permission, for dogs, from dogs.

Play-bow. Down on the front elbows with the rump in the air. Dogs do this when inviting a friend to play with them.

Chapter Six

The Empty Car

The next day, we came to a place where the road split in different directions. A wooden signpost stood with one arm pointing back the way we'd come. James looked at his map. "Guess this is the place Mick called the five-way, Stamp," he said to me. "Only I think I see six tracks, so there's no real middle one."

He got out and walked up and down, looking at the different routes. "A signpost pointing where we want to go instead of where we came from would be useful," he said. Then he bent and looked at the ground. "No wheel marks, either. All that rain would have washed old tracks away. We'll try the third track and if it's wrong, we'll have to come back."

He got back into the Fourby and we started off again.

After a bit, Ace scrabbled at the window. "Want to stop."

"We just started," I said.

"*Need* to stop," said Ace, and scratched the back of James's seat.

We stopped, and James walked us around until Ace made a puddle. I found a stubby tree trunk and cocked my leg against it. The trees out here were all stubby, but there was a lot of long grass and bushes, and some big rocks. There were interesting tracks in the grass. I smelled wallabies and some sort of lizard. Ace yapped at a couple of black cockatoos and tried to catch a grasshopper.

We were heading back to the Fourby when I saw something shining out from under one of the stunted trees. I stopped for another look.

"Come on, Stamp," said James, clicking his fingers. Normally I do what James says, but I hadn't had a good run since we left Billabong Camp and I didn't want to get back into the Fourby yet. I tugged back and pointed my muzzle towards the shiny thing.

"What's that?" I said.

Ace looked where I was looking. "Something shiny," she said. She sniffed the breeze. "Not water."

"Now what?" James asked. He turned

to see what we were looking at, and of-paws he saw it, too. "Some old wreck," he said. "Let's go and have a quick look."

As we got closer, I saw it was a car. It was gray with dust and the windows were dirty, but it wasn't a wreck. It was parked right under the tree, but a bit of sunlight must have shone on the metal.

We went right up to it and I sniffed at one of the tires. James used both hands to shade his eyes while he tried to look in through the window.

"Can't see much," he said. He walked around the back of the car. "Kookaburra Rentals, Perth. And it's a Western Australia **license plate**." He tried one of the doors, but it must have been locked. "Hello?" he called, and banged on the glass. "Hello?"

Ace thought that was a good game, so she started yapping.

James called out a few more times, then shrugged and shook his head. "Maybe whoever it is ran out of gas," he said. "Could be those lost tourists, but surely they'd know to stay with the car? I'd better **call it in**." Then he looked at his watch. "No, it's too early for **the band** to be open. Have to wait for a few hours."

On our way back to the Fourby, Ace stopped again. She sniffed hard. "Socks," she said to me. She ducked her head into the long grass and came up holding a round bundle of cloth. She was right. It was a pair of socks.

"Thank you, Ace." James bent and held out his hand. "Give it to me, please."

Ace gave the bundled socks a good shake and dropped them into James's hand. Then she smarled smugly. "I found a clue."

"Socks," said James, looking at the bundle.

Ace sniffed the ground. "They went *that* way," she said.

Stamp's Glossary

The band. Frequency range for radios.
Call it in. Report something by radio.
License plate. The license plates on a vehicle show which state it came from.

Chapter Seven

Danger in the Grass

Ace wanted to follow the scent, but James had other ideas. He is usually sensible, but I **suppaws** he didn't realize that Ace had picked up the trail from the socks. We dogs have a much better sense of smell than humans. If we smell someone's clothing, we can often follow their trail. Shoes and socks are very good for carrying scent.

James made us go back to the Fourby.

He checked the time again, then tried to
call Dad Barnaby on the HF radio. The
band didn't seem to be open yet.

James opened the back of the Fourby
and rigged up a shade cloth. He got us
a drink of water and made some coffee,
then settled down with a book. He didn't
say much to us. I suppaws he was worried
about the empty car.

Ace edged up towards the steaming
mug. James grabbed her collar. "No, Ace.
You'll burn your nose."

Ace sat down to have a good scratch. I pottered around, sniffing the Fourby's tires. After a bit, we moved away from the car. James didn't call us back, so of-paws we trotted back to the empty car. We had **unfinished business** with that trail of scent.

When we got there, we **cast about** near the car. Now that we'd gotten a whiff of the right scent, I could smell it along the edge of the car door. I didn't know whose scent it was, of-paws, but I knew it was the person who had carried the socks. The funny thing was, the scent

didn't head for the road where the Fourby was. It went off in the other direction, along a faint, dusty track. It didn't seem like a human track to me. It was more like something made by kangaroos or wombats. We crossed over James's scent and our own, and that confused us both. Ace went off while I was still checking which way we'd gone before.

"I smell something," said Ace. She drilled her sharp little nose into the ground and sniffed. Then she sneezed so hard her ears waggled.

I just said, "Of-paws you do. We smelled it earlier." I should have been more alert.

Ace started off the dusty track and into some longer grass. "It's going this way," she reported. "Oh, here it is—wiggly thing—"

That's when I heard a dry rustle in the grass. Not only that, I saw something moving. It looked like a long piece of hose being pulled along, but it wasn't a hose. It was a snake.

Now, most snakes don't attack unless someone bothers them. Sensible dogs back off when they see snakes, but when dogs like Ace suddenly see something moving, they will sometimes just rush in and grab. That's terrier-ably dangerous, but I didn't have time to explain that to Ace. Besides, Ace had started yapping and yaffling with excitement, so she wouldn't have heard me anyway. I did the only thing I could think of. I pounced on Ace before she could pounce on the snake.

"Stop!" I dashed forward and grabbed Ace by the scruff of the neck. Of-paws, she twisted around and bit my elbow.

I yelped. As soon as I opened my mouth and let go, Ace launched herself at my ear and latched on with her sharp teeth. It really hurt and I yelped again and shook my head. Ace just hung on, so I snarled and tried to grab her.

She snarled too. I'm a lot bigger and stronger than Ace, and I have bigger teeth, but she had a good grip on my ear and she was furious. She thought I'd attacked her for no reason. We were both

making so much noise that I didn't realize James was there until a jet of water hit me in the eye. James had squirted me with the spray bottle he uses for cleaning the Fourby windows.

"Stop that!" James dropped the spray bottle, threw his jacket over Ace and hung on with one hand while he locked the other around her muzzle. She let go of my ear right away and yelped with shock.

"You are *not* to do that!" James made his voice really deep and growly so we knew he meant it. Ace tucked her tail between her legs and I shook my head. My ear stung and I whined when James felt it.

"Honestly!" grumbled James. "I take my eye off the two of you for five minutes and you start fighting! What's *wrong* with you today?"

Ace gave me a dirty look. "You started it." Her sharp little teeth were still bared in a snarl.

"I was saving you from the snake," I said. "That long wiggly thing you were about to bite might have bitten *you*. You could have been very sick or even died."

"So you bit me instead!" muttered Ace, but she dropped her lip. Then she came close to me and reached up to lick my face. "Sorry about your ear," she said.

I licked her back. "If you'd just listen before you jump . . ."

Ace sniffed.

"You two . . ." warned James.

We looked at him and then at each other.

"Be nice," I said quickly to Ace. "He thinks we were just fighting and if we're not careful, we'll end up leashed in the back of the Fourby."

Ace play-bowed. I did it too and wagged my tail. We pretended to play a little game.

"That's better," said James with a relieved smile. "I suppose you were playing and someone got a bit rough."

Ace and I exchanged glances. Even the best of humans get things wrong sometimes.

"What's so interesting about this place, anyway?" asked James. "Is this where you found the socks?"

He took the socks out of his pocket and held them down to our level. Ace and I sniffed hard, then we cast about. This time, I found the trail, leading off beyond where Ace found the snake.

James looked back to where the Fourby was parked. Then he came up beside me. "Okay, Stamp, where to now? You've obviously got the scent of something."

"This way!" yapped Ace, shooting ahead of me. She stopped to spit something black out in the grass. It was a tuft of hair off my left ear. Suddenly, I felt quite cross.

Stamp's Glossary

Cast about. Trotting back and forth, looking for a clue.
Suppaws. Suppose, for dogs.
Unfinished business. Something impawtant or interesting that still needs attention.

A Word about
Snakes and Spiders

Snakes, spiders, wasps and bees and other venomous creatures are dangerous to dogs, just as they are to humans. Many dogs are curious about things that move suddenly and will go to investigate or even try to catch them. Don't let your dogs roam off-leash during snake season, and if you know wasps or venomous spiders are around, try to keep your dogs away. Clean up trash and debris where spiders may hide. If you know or suspect your dog has been bitten or stung, get them to the vet as soon as you can.

Chapter Eight

The Map

James took some rope out of his pocket and tied it to our collars, then fastened us to two stout shrubs. "Sit. Wait." He looked at his compass. "Due west," he muttered, then turned and jogged back towards the Fourby.

"He's not cross enough to leave us here is he?" Ace started to **nose-whinge** which is a very annoying noise.

"No!" I snapped. "Of-*paws* not. He'll

be right back." I licked my elbow, which was sore, although not as sore as my ear.

Ace sat down and stared after James.

"Look," I said, "he's coming back. I think he went to get supplies."

James had brought his backpack and a **canteen**. I heard water sloshing in it and licked my dry lips.

He poured a bit of water into his hand for me and Ace, then untied us. "Okay . . . track . . . sniff . . . follow," he said. Then he laughed. "That's what you were doing anyway, right?"

He followed us for a long way, calling Ace back when she got too far ahead. I noticed she paid attention to him this time. Every so often he'd stop and check the direction on his compass. Then he'd call out, "*Coooo-ee!*" making the end of the word slide up high. It made my ears ring, so I expect the sound carried a long way in the still air.

We didn't know the name of the people we were tracking, but I knew there were two of them. One was the person who had dropped the socks. The other one smelled different. They were walking along together.

Then I found something else. It was a big piece of paper folded up to about the size of the long envelopes Dad Barnaby gets from the post office back home. I barked because it smelled like the second person we were tracking.

"What have you got?" James picked up the paper. He unfolded it and I realized it was a map, like the one James had back at the Fourby.

"Hey . . ." James rubbed my ears. "Good boy, Stamp."

My ear was still sore, so I pulled my head away and wagged my tail instead.

James spread the map out on the ground and traced it with his finger. "It's been penciled in," he said. "Whoever it belongs to must have come through from the Karumba turnoff, through Wahwee Creek. I suppose they were avoiding the floodwater, the same as we are." Then he frowned. "I have no idea why they'd be walking this way, though. It's *away* from the road, unless there's another one not marked on the map?"

He folded the map and tucked it under his arm. "Better not go too much farther. The band will be open soon and if people are wandering around out here . . ." He didn't finish his sentence, but I knew snakes and bulldust weren't the only dangerous things in the outback. "Another five minutes," he decided.

We set off again.

The trouble with tracking something through the empty open country like this was there was no obvious place to stop and turn around. Ace and I were following a trail we could smell, but all James could do was to follow us. "Next tree," he kept saying, but then he'd see another one in the distance and say, "next tree," again.

"Right, at the next tree, we really *will* turn around," he finally said. "There's no point in us getting lost as well." But the next tree turned out to be a whole little clump of trees, and they looked a lot greener than most of the others.

"Cooo-ee!" yelled James, and coughed. I expect his throat was getting dry. I know mine was.

Then I pricked up my ears. Was that a noise from up ahead? A cockatoo, maybe?

I listened again. Then Ace yapped and darted off towards the clump of trees.

Three kangaroos bounced past and Ace **jinked** sideways to chase them.

"Ace, *stop*!" yelled James.

And Ace did stop. She dropped her tail

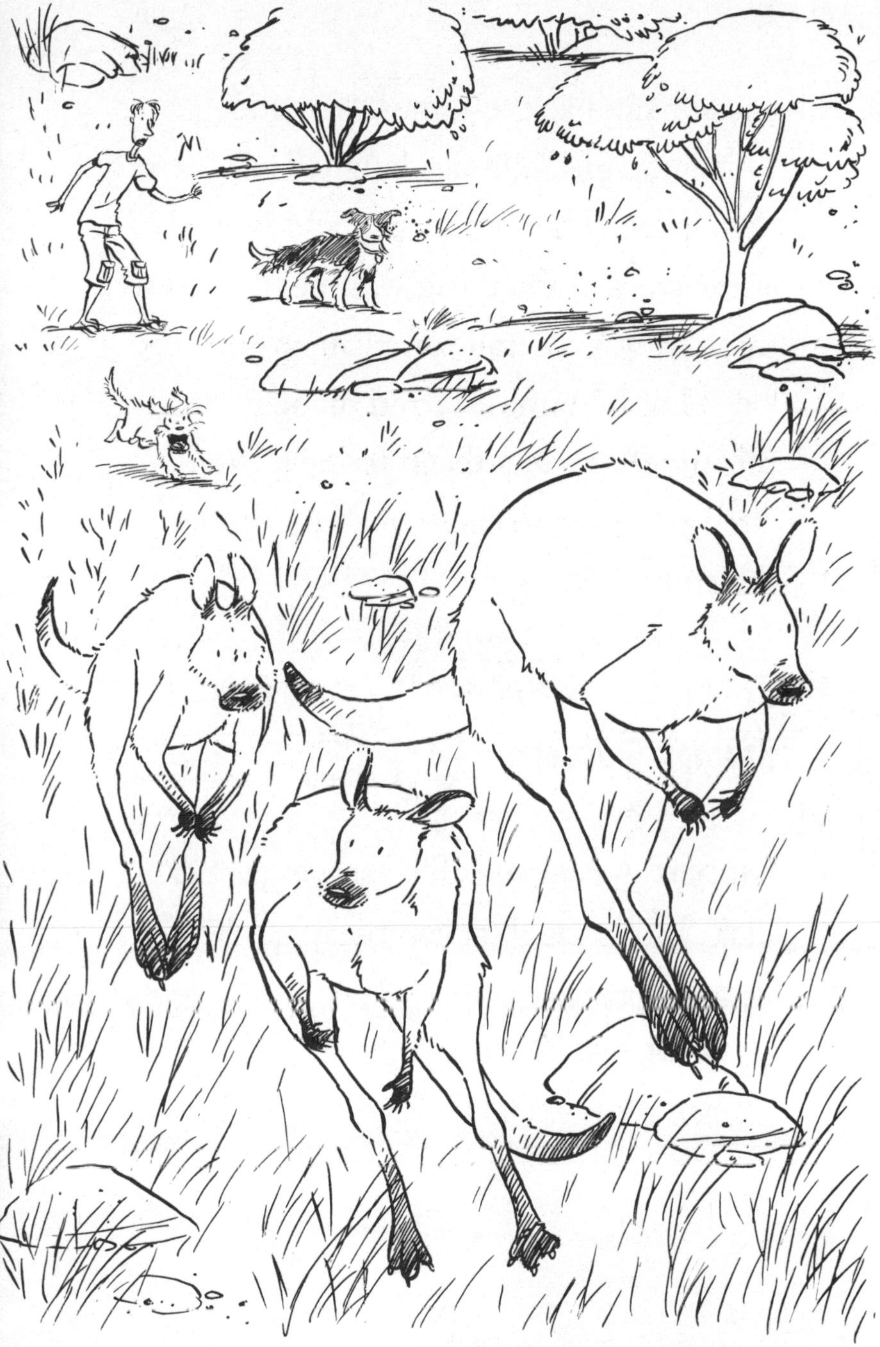

and slinked back to James. "Treat?"

"Good girl." James laughed and gave
her a treat. Then he turned and looked
at the trees. Something was moving over
there. It was too tall for a kangaroo.

"Hello?" James started off again, and
this time I trotted ahead to meet the
strange man who came out from under
the trees.

Stamp's Glossary

Canteen. A container for carrying water.
Jink. To change direction really quickly
when running.
Nose-whinge. A really annoying high-
pitched whine.

Chapter Nine

Elsa and Fritz

"Hello?" said the man. He was older than James and he seemed really glad to see us.

"Hello." James coughed again. "Sorry, I've been calling out."

"We thought we heard someone, as well as a dog!" The man held out his hand. "So glad to see you." He turned back to the trees. "**Liebling**? Elsa? We are rescued!" He faced James again. "Please. My wife has sore feet from shoes."

"Blisters?" James asked.

"**Ja**, blisters."

James took the socks out of his pocket. "Are these her socks? My dogs found them back near your car."

"Ja! Ja!" The man laughed. "Clever dogs!"

Ace yipped and capered around, putting her paws on the man's knee.

"Ja, little one. It is good to see you, too," said the man. "My name is Fritz Mueller," he said to James. "And Elsa and I have not been clever, I think."

Elsa was waiting for us in the shade of the trees. There was a little **soak** there, and she sat beside it with her shoes off. She looked up and smiled when we came up. "You are part of a rescue party?" she said when James had introduced us.

"No, we *are* the rescue party," said

James. "My dogs spotted your car when we stopped back on the road, and then they found your socks and a map you must have dropped. My dad said there were tourists missing up here, so we followed your trail. But why were you walking away from the road?"

Fritz made a twirling motion with his fingers. "We put the headlights on to drive through the big dust and *ach!* I forgot to turn them off. The battery, it went . . . *pffft!*" He sighed. "No spare. Very bad."

"We walk back to the road to find other cars," put in Elsa.

"We *think* we walk back to the road," said Fritz.

"I see," said James. "It's really easy to get lost out here."

"Then Elsa gets . . . blister? Ja? And

we found this water."

"It's a good place to be, since you found shade and water," said James, "although it would have been better to stay with the car."

"I know. We lost car also."

Elsa clicked her fingers to us. "Dear dogs," she said. "We plan to get a dog when we go home to Liepzig. A good handsome dog like this fellow." She scrubbed my neck.

"Or a little **niedlich** dog like this, ja?" Fritz scratched

Ace on the tummy and she **grungled**.

James sat down and opened his canteen, and then took some supplies from his backpack. "It's all camping food," he said. "Fresh food doesn't stay very fresh when you're traveling, but I have nuts and cookies."

"**Wunderbar**!" said Elsa.

"I have a first aid kit, too," said James. He handed it to Elsa.

"But what now?" asked Fritz when they had eaten some food and bandaged Elsa's feet. "Are you lost, too?"

"No, I have a compass, and besides, Ace and Stamp will know how to get back to our car," said James. "It's a long walk, so if you'd rather I left you here and went back to radio for help . . ."

"No, no!" said Elsa. "We can walk. I have had enough of this place."

Stamp's Glossary

Grungle. A happy little growl.
Liebling. Darling, in German. Say it *leeb-ling.*
Ja. Yes, in German. Say it *yah.*
Niedlich. Cute, in German. Say it *need-lick.*
Soak. A small spring.
Wunderbar. Wonderful, in German. Say it *voon-da-bar.*

Chapter Ten
Wunderbar!

We had to walk slowly because of Elsa's sore feet, but everyone was happy, so it didn't matter. Fritz even carried Ace part of the way. Of-paws she can walk a long way, but he said she was a **kluge kleine socken hund**.

Ace snuggled into Fritz's arms and stared down at me. "I'm higher than you, Stamp," she smarled.

I paid no attention. Elsa kept asking

James questions about me, so I felt impawtant too. "Is it his breed that makes Stamp so clever?" she asked.

"Border collies are clever dogs," said James, "but Ace is a little mix and she is very clever, too." Then he told Fritz and Elsa all about how we came to be traveling together.

As he walked, James kept checking his compass, but I kept my nose on our trail from time to time, just in case.

We came back to the rental car first, and stopped so Elsa could sit down.

"Do you have enough gas to get back to the main road?" asked James.

"We carry extra in spare cans," said Fritz. "Only the battery is *pfft*."

"I have **jumper cables** in the Fourby," said James. "If you like, I can try jump-starting your car so you can drive out

instead of waiting for a tow truck."

"*Wunderbar!*" exclaimed Fritz.

James left us with Fritz and Elsa while he went to fetch the Fourby. The Muellers kept shaking their heads over how close they had been to the road and wondering how they could have gone the wrong way. Apparently, they had driven off the road and out under the tree when they set up camp for the night. They had a camping lantern and they hadn't noticed the headlights were still on when they went to sleep in their tent.

In the morning, they packed up their camp and got in the car to drive back to the road. That was when they discovered that the car's battery was dead. They decided to walk to the road to get some help, but then they got lost.

While we waited for James, Ace and

I got a lot of attention and praise for our part in the rescue. It felt good.

James drove back carefully, and then he and Fritz got to work attaching jumper cables to the rental car. Soon they had it going again. James made sure it was fully charged.

Before Fritz and Elsa left us, James called Dad Barnaby on the HF radio.

"Hi, Dad. You remember those lost tourists you told me about? Over."

"Yes," said Dad Barnaby. "What about them, James? Over."

"We found them," said James. "Their car had a dead battery, but they're okay. Can you get in touch with the authorities and tell them Fritz and Elsa Mueller are driving back to the highway via Billabong Camp?" He said the names again slowly so Dad Barnaby could write them down.

"Will do," said Dad Barnaby. Then he started laughing. "I thought you were sticking to the main road, James? Over."

"We didn't get lost," laughed James. "We just took a detour. And now we're headed to Wahwee Creek . . ." Then, quietly, so Dad Barnaby couldn't hear, he added, "That's if we can find it . . ."

We said good-bye to Fritz and Elsa, and they wrote down our address at Barnaby Station and promised to keep in touch.

"We will send you a picture of our so-beautiful pedigreed dog when we get him," said Elsa, hugging me and slipping me a biscuit.

"Ja, or our funny clever socks dog from the rescue home," said Fritz, rubbing Ace's tummy while she waved her paws in the air.

We watched them drive back the way we had come, towards Billabong Camp.

Weeks later, Fritz and Elsa sent James a letter with a photograph. James read it aloud to us.

Dear James, Stamp and Ace,

Thank you much again for rescuing us when we lost ourselves in your beautiful country. We are home again now and we still think of you all. Last week we went to choose a dog to join our family. Here is our picture of what happened next. Isn't it wunderbar?

With love to you all,
Fritz, Elsa, Ada and Strom.

"Well!" James sounded *very* pleased. "Well, look at that!" He showed us the photo. In it Fritz and Elsa were holding *two* dogs—one handsome young border collie and one rough-coated little terrier mix!

"*Wunderbar!*" yelled James.

Ace smarled smugly. "Because of us, two more dogs have a home." She sniffed. "I wonder if *they* are allowed to go henning?"

As for me, I gave our outback adventure my biggest **stamp of approval**!

Stamp's Glossary

Jumper cables. Cables that let you transfer the power of one car battery to another.
Kluge kleine socken hund. Clever little socks dog, in German. Say it *clue-ga cline-a zocken hoond*.
Stamp of approval. An award of honor. Only I can give it.

A Word on Choosing a Dog

When you choose a dog to join your family, think about the kind of dog you want. If you love going out and about, consider a dog that likes exercise and company. If you are more of a curl-up-in-a-chair person, choose a dog that enjoys a lot of rest. Whatever kind of dog you want, remember that puppies grow up. Every dog has a different personality. All dogs need care and attention, so plan carefully.

Catch Stamp, Ace and James in their other Pup Patrol adventures!

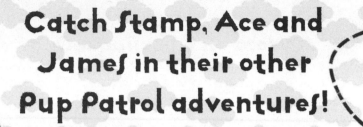